D0792096

For all of my friends at Apple

First edition 2020

Library of Congress Catalog Card Number pending

ISBN 978-1-5362-0491-9

20 21 22 23 24 25 CCP 10 9 8 7 6 5 4 3 2 1

Printed in Shenzhen, Guangdong, China

This book was typeset in Alghera.
The illustrations were done in watercolor and ink.

Candlewick Press
99 Dover Street
Somerville, Massachusetts 02144

www.candlewick.com

Miss Mingo

and the 100th Day of School

Jamie Harper

Candlewick Press

The day began as usual in Miss Mingo's class.
But this was no usual day!

6	7	8	9	10
16	17	18	19	20
26	27	28	29	30
36	37	38	39	40
46	47	48	49	50
56	57	58	59	60
66	67	68	69	70
76	77	78	79	80
86	87	88	89	90
96	97	98	99	100

WEATHER

February

14

"We made it!" shouted
Monkey. "One hundred
days of school!"

"One hundred is a big
number, so we will celebrate
BIG," said Miss Mingo.

The class whooped and hollered.
"Let's begin with a tour of your 100th Day
projects," said Miss Mingo.

"Hippo, why don't you go first, since your mom just arrived," she said.

"My sister weighs 100 pounds," said Hippo. "And she was just born yesterday."

Hippo calves can nurse underwater by closing their ears and nostrils.

"Who knew?" said Pig. "That baby is as big as *me!*"

"Congratulations!" said Miss Mingo. She called on Octopus next.

"I picked these shells out of our garden," he said.

"How do you know there are 100?" asked Miss Mingo.

"I made 10 piles with 10 shells in each one," answered Octopus.

"Good thinking—a stupendous strategy," said Miss Mingo.

After dining on crabs, clams, shrimp, and lobster, an octopus tosses the empty shells outside its den in piles commonly called octopus's gardens.

"I got to 100 in a different way, Miss Mingo," said Panda.
"I counted out 50 stalks of bamboo and made a bundle;
then I made a second one the same way."
"Great job!" said Miss Mingo. "Two groups of 50 equal 100."

Pandas' favorite food is bamboo.
They can eat up to 40 pounds
a day! They eat the leaves and
roots, but the tender green shoots
are especially tasty.

The class followed Cricket to the board, where she
showed off her drawing skills.

"My dad has 100 itty-bitty teeth on one wing," she said.
"He rubs it against the other wing when he wants to chirp."

scraper

teeth

file

my dad!

Male crickets chirp by rubbing the scraper of one forewing on the comb-like file of the other; this process is called stridulation.

Miss Mingo felt a tug on one of her feathers.

"I left my project at home," said Cockroach.

"Oh, dear," said Miss Mingo. "Let's see if we can come up with a project in the classroom. Why don't you pick 100 leaves from one of our plants?"

Cockroach couldn't believe his good luck! Maybe he could sneak a few bites. After all, eating was his favorite thing to do.

Then he smelled the plant. It was mint! "YUCK!"

Cockroaches eat just about anything, but they detest the smell of mint—and of other herbs such as rosemary, bay leaves, and catnip.

"Poor Cockroach," said Koala. "One of my teddy bears will make you feel better. I've got 99 more. Everyone gives me teddy bears because they think I'm a bear. But I'm not."

Out came all the toy bears.

Some had tea.

Some went for a ride.

A bunch got a big squeeze.

Koalas are marsupials, which means females have a pouch in which they carry their young until they are about six months old.

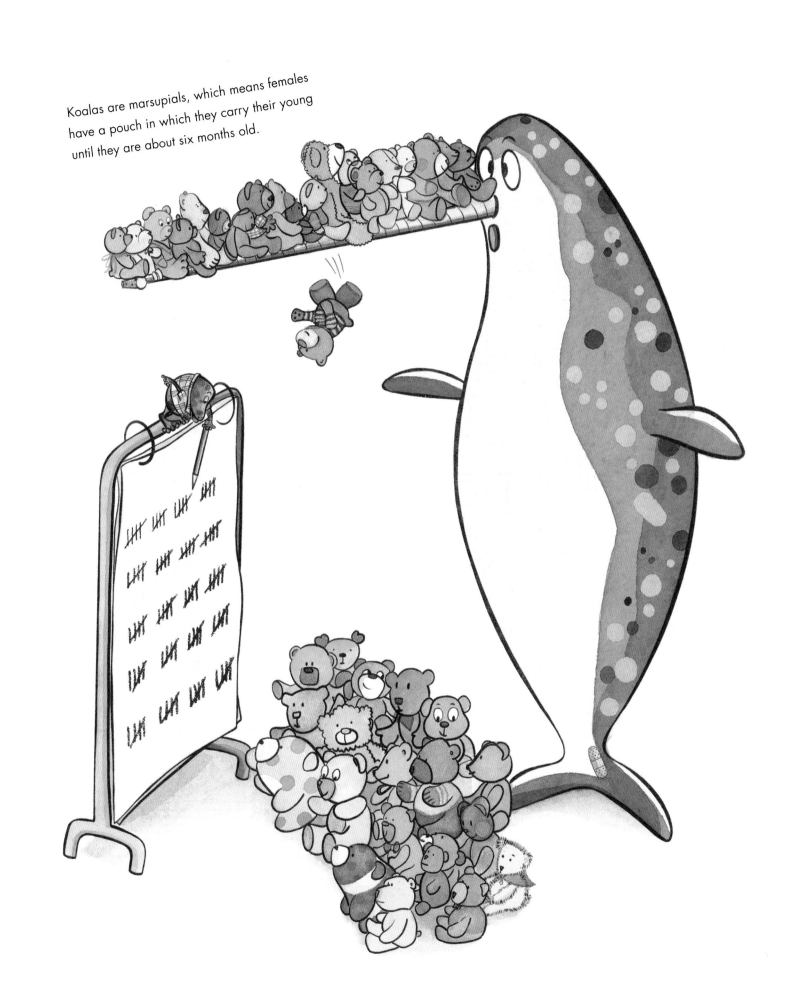

The class needed to get back on track, and Miss Mingo knew that Centipede's project would do the trick. "Naturally, all these legs make me a great athlete," said Centipede. "I can do 100 jumping jacks! Can you?" she challenged her classmates.

Centipedes are fast and agile. House centipedes can travel 15 inches (38 centimeters) per second. That's like a person running 58 feet (18 meters) in a second!

"What a workout, Centipede," said Miss Mingo.
"It must be 100 degrees in here."
"No, it's around 80 degrees," said Monkey,
"but that's almost 100."

Proboscis monkeys live
near rivers or streams on
the island of Borneo, where
it's very hot and humid.

"How many more degrees would make
100?" asked Miss Mingo.
"Twenty more!" her students shouted,
huffing and puffing.

After recess, Pig noticed someone new in the room.

"Panda, is that your dad?" asked Koala.

"Maybe it's a monster," cried Pig.

"Don't be ridiculous," said Alligator. "It's a cow."

"Guys, it's me," Narwhal said. "I dressed up as Granny, the famous orca. Some scientists think she lived to be more than 100 years old."

Granny, also known as J2, was the matriarch of a pod of orcas in the Pacific Northwest that biologists studied for more than forty years. She was last sighted in October 2016.

"Miss Mingo, I'm stressed out," said Alligator. "Could I go next? One hundred seconds of deep breathing every day makes me feel more confident, connected, and inspired."

When the air is cooler than about 70°F (21°C), alligators may stay submerged for hours or even days, breathing through their snouts, which they hold above the surface.

Alligator demonstrated some yoga positions. A few students joined in.

The room was still and peaceful. The perfect time, Miss Mingo thought, for the group project to be displayed. "Five of us got together and we made 20 footprints each—or belly prints, in Snake's case!"

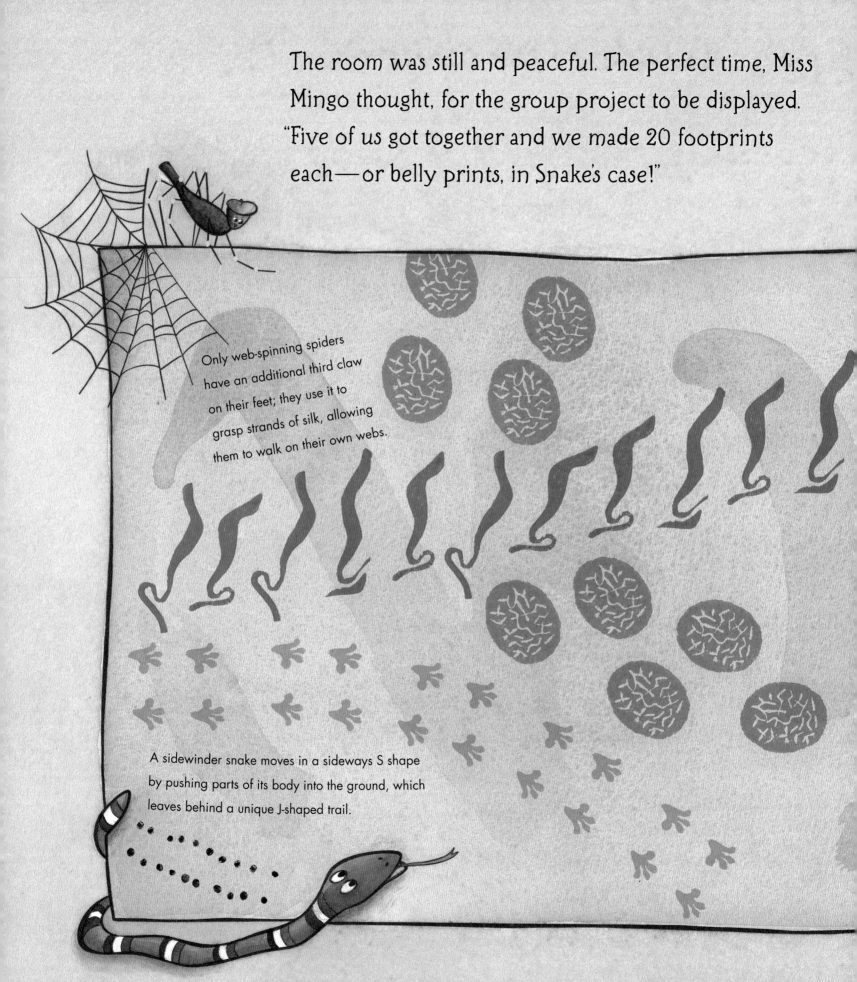

Only web-spinning spiders have an additional third claw on their feet; they use it to grasp strands of silk, allowing them to walk on their own webs.

A sidewinder snake moves in a sideways S shape by pushing parts of its body into the ground, which leaves behind a unique J-shaped trail.

"Can you figure out which prints belong to me, Bird, Snake, Elephant, and Spider?"

Perching birds can sleep safely on a thin branch or wire thanks to a pulley system of tendons in their legs that lock their toes tightly into place.

Because of the structure of their feet, elephants actually walk on their tiptoes.

Sticky pads on the toes of tree frogs make them excellent climbers. Mucus secreted from the pads removes dirt from their paths for even better traction.

"I'm wearing my project," said Giraffe at lunchtime.

"I know," said Koala. "You have 100 spots."

"Well, sort of," said Giraffe. "There are 100 on one side and 100 on the other."

No two giraffes have the same spot patterns.
As giraffes get older, their spots grow darker.

"I can dive into the ocean from 100 feet in the air,"
said Pelican. "See?"

"Mercy, do you wear a helmet when you dive?" asked
Miss Dillo, the lunch monitor.

"Don't worry, Miss Dillo," said Pelican. "My body is built
for big plunges."

Air sacs under brown pelicans' skin act like cushions and protect them when they hit the water.

Meanwhile, Ant and 99 of his buddies were making sure no potato chips went to waste.

Ants rely on teamwork to move heavy objects;
they take turns carrying, steering, and leading.

Groundhog wandered in, looking a little sleepy.

"Did I miss lunch?" he asked.

"Where have you been?" asked Alligator.

"Sleeping," said Groundhog. "I just woke up from my
100-day nap."

Groundhogs live in underground burrows complete with
sleeping chambers, nursery chambers, and toilet chambers.

"Come over here," said Miss Dillo.
"I have a project, too! I knitted
gifts for my 100 favorite relatives.
They're playing outside now."
Everyone ran to the window.
They all whooped and hollered.

"Whoa," said Frog. "You're a good knitter, Miss Dillo."

Nine-banded armadillos almost always have four identical same-gender pups in a litter.

Before the 100th Day celebration was over, Miss Mingo made two requests:

work in teams to build something with 100 paper cups . . .

and make a silly face for 100 seconds.

"Congratulations, class," said Miss Mingo, "on 100 days of success."

"And 100 days of learning," said Panda.

"Plus 100 days of hard work," said Frog.

"Not to mention 100 days of having the best teacher ever," said Hippo.

And the 100th day of school ended with 100 marching steps out of the classroom while Bird sang a song.